D0166796

Hey Jack! Books

The Crazy Cousins
The Scary Solo
The Winning Goal
The Robot Blues
The Worry Monsters
The New Friend
The Worst Sleepover
The Circus Lesson
The Bumpy Ride
The Top Team
The Playground Problem
The Best Party Ever
The Bravest Kid
The Big Adventure
The Toy Sale

First American Edition 2013
Kane Miller, A Division of EDC Publishing

Text copyright © 2013 Sally Rippin
Illustration copyright © 2013 Stephanie Spartels
Logo and design copyright © 2013 Hardie Grant Egmont

First published in Australia in 2013 by Hardie Grant Egmont

For information contact:
Kane Miller, A Division of EDC Publishing
P.O. Box 470663
Tulsa, OK 74147-0663
www.kanemiller.com
www.edcpub.com
www.usbornebooksandmore.com

Library of Congress Control Number: 2012956114

Printed and bound in the United States of America
6 7 8 9 10
ISBN: 978-1-61067-187-3

The Bumpy Ride

By Sally Rippin

Illustrated by Stephanie Spartels

Kane Miller
A DIVISION OF EDC PUBLISHING

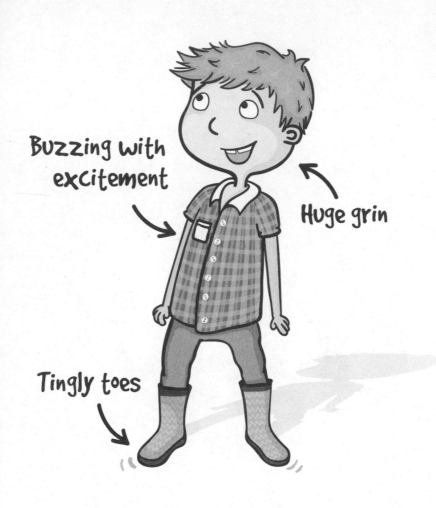

Buzzing with excitement

Huge grin

Tingly toes

Fizzy Mood

Chapter One

This is Jack.

Today Jack is in a
fizzy mood. He is
as fizzy and whizzy
as a firecracker.

Jack and Billie are going horseback riding!

Jack is so excited he feels like he might **explode**.

Billie and Jack are in a camp program. Yesterday they made pasta necklaces. Pasta necklaces aren't nearly as exciting as horseback riding.

Today, Billie and Jack
have dressed up like
cowboys.

It is a long drive to the horseback riding place. Billie and Jack sit at the back of the bus. They sing a song that they made up with their camp program friends:

"I'm riding my horse on the range — YEE-HAW!

I'm rounding up all of the cows – YEE-HAW!

I'm hot and I'm dusty and tired – YEE-HAW!

I'm a cow…"

When they get to this bit, the boys sing "BOY!" and the girls sing "GIRL!" as **loudly** as they can.

The camp program leaders, Cindy and Kwan, are at the front of the bus.

"OK, kids," Cindy says. "Maybe you can sing something quieter now?"

Jack and Billie **giggle**.

Finally they get to the horseback riding place. Jack and Billie get off the bus.

Then they all go
together to the stables.
Jack is so excited that he
runs the whole way.

A man on a big black
horse **trots** over.
"Hey there!" he says.
"My name is Jim.
And this is my horse,
Lightning." He swings
down onto the ground.

Wow. He looks super cool!
Jack thinks. *Just like a
real cowboy.*

"So, who's ridden a
horse before?" Jim asks.

Billie puts up her hand.
So do lots of other
kids. Jack begins to feel
worried. He's never
ridden a horse before.

Jim matches everyone
with a horse. Billie gets
a speckled gray horse
called Fury. It looks cool.
Billie looks very proud.

"Anybody not have a

horse yet?" Jim calls out.

Jack puts up his hand.
"Not me," he says quietly.
"I haven't ridden before."

"That doesn't matter,
pal!" Jim says. He pats
Jack's shoulder. "I have
just the horse for you."

Jim takes Jack over to
the last stable.

Inside is a brown horse with a **fat** belly. She is munching straw.

"This is Betty," says Jim. "She'll be perfect for a beginner."

Jack sighs. He was hoping for a big black horse like Lightning. Or at least a speckled gray horse like Fury.

Not a fat brown pony

called Betty!

Chapter Two

Jim helps everyone put
a saddle on their horse.
Jack and Jim can hardly
do Betty's saddle up
because she is so fat!

Finally they get it done. But now Jack is feeling very hot and **dusty**.

Next, Jim tells Jack to lead Betty out of the stable. Billie's horse trots out easily. But stubborn old Betty won't budge!

Jack looks up at Jim.
"Can't I have a different
horse?" he whispers.

Jim chuckles. "Betty
is a good pony, pal.
Trust me."

No, she's not, Jack thinks. *I
got the* **worst** *pony of all!*

Jim helps Jack lead
Betty outside. Everyone
is waiting for them.
Jack sighs.

Jim shows them how
to get on a horse.
He puts his left foot
in the stirrup, and then
swings his right leg
over Lightning's back.

"Now you try," says Jim.

Jack puts one foot in the
stirrup. Then he hops up
and down for a minute.

He is feeling a little

nervous.

Just as he is about to
swing his other foot over,
Betty trots forward. Jack
falls onto his bottom.
Right in the mud!

Everyone laughs. Jack feels his cheeks get **hot** with embarrassment.

 "Not to worry!" says Jim, helping Jack up. "You look like a real cowboy now. You'll never see a clean cowboy, that's for sure!"

"I guess," mumbles Jack.

Finally he gets onto Betty's back.

All the horses start moving forward. Billie's horse moves very **quickly**. It tries to get up to the front.

"Wait for me!" Jack calls.

"I can't help it!" Billie calls back. "Sorry!"

Betty trudges along at the very back of the line. Sometimes she even stops to munch on grass.

"Oh, you are SO annoying!" Jack says. "I wish I had Billie's horse!"

He tries to make Betty go faster, but she just goes at her own pace.

Jim takes them for a ride through the woods. They go up hills and down hills. They even **splash** through a stream!

Jack feels annoyed that he has the slowest horse, but he still has a good time.

Jack tries to see where Billie is, but she's too far ahead. Suddenly he hears her cry out.

Oh no, Jack thinks.

Billie's in trouble!

Chapter Three

Betty and Jack finally
catch up to Billie. Jim
is holding Billie's horse
by the reins. Its eyes are
white and **wild**.

31

Jack hops off Betty.

Billie has dirty tears all down her cheeks. Cindy is kneeling next to her.

When Billie sees Jack,
she bursts into tears again.

"What happened?"
Jack asks.

Kwan frowns. "Billie's
horse isn't behaving
today. She got a
fright and tipped
poor Billie off."

Billie shows Jack a big

muddy scrape all down

one arm.

34

Oh, how scary! Jack thinks. *I'm glad I wasn't riding her horse.*

"I said I would ride back with Billie to help her clean up," Cindy says. "But Billie is too scared to get back onto her horse.

And Jim needs to
look after the group."

"We need someone
with a nice gentle
horse who can go
with Cindy and Billie,"
explains Kwan.

Jack looks at Jim.

Jim smiles and nods.

"I'll do it!" Jack says.
"Billie can ride with me."

"That's very kind of you, Jack," says Cindy. "Are you sure your horse won't do anything silly?"

Jack leans over and pats Betty's mane.

"Nah," he says. "Betty wouldn't hurt a fly. Would you, girl?"

Then he looks back at Jim, who winks at him.

"Thanks, Jack," says Billie. She wipes her eyes on her sleeve.

Cindy helps Billie up onto Betty's saddle behind Jack. Betty stands very still. Jack is sure she understands that she needs to be on her best behavior.

"Good girl," he says
quietly.

"I knew you and

Betty would make

a good team,"

Jim says, watching.

"I keep her for

special people.

And, like me, Betty

can always spot a

true cowboy when

she sees one."

Jack grins. Even though he is hot and dusty and dirty, he has never felt so proud.

Collect them all!